S0-BYF-642

DATE DUE

118960 EN
One More Chance

Robins, Eleanor
ATOS BL 2.7
Points: 1.0   UG

ONE MORE CHANCE

By Eleanor Robins

Development: Kent Publishing Services, Inc.
Design and Production: Signature Design Group, Inc.
Illustrations: Jan Naimo Jones

SADDLEBACK EDUCATIONAL PUBLISHING
Three Watson
Irvine, CA 92618-2767

Website: www.sdlback.com

ISBN-13: 978-1-56254-774-5
ISBN 1-56254-774-7
eBook: 978-1-60291-070-6

Printed in the United States of America

12 11 10 09 08 9 8 7 6 5 4 3

Chapter 1

June stood in front of the school. June talked to Rose. Rose was her best friend. It was almost time for school to start.

June was on the volleyball team. Rose was on the team too. They had a match after school. It was their first big match. Carter High would play Hillman High.

June asked, "Are you excited about playing Hillman High, Rose? I am."

"Yes," Rose said.

"Do you think we can beat Hillman High?" June asked.

"I don't know. Hillman High has a very good team," Rose said.

Marge came over to June and Rose. Marge was in June's math class.

Marge said, "Good luck today."

"Thanks," Rose said.

"Do you think Carter High will win?" Marge asked.

"Yes," June said.

Marge asked, "Are you sure, June? I know we have won all of our matches. But the other teams weren't very good. Hillman High has a very good team."

"I am sure we will win," June said.

But June wasn't really sure they would win.

Carter High played four teams. The teams didn't play well. And Carter High was 4–0. But Hillman High played well. Hillman High was 4–0 too.

Marge said, "Look, June. Zack is over there. He is talking to Kim."

Zack had been June's boyfriend last year. But he got very upset with her, and he broke up with her. They had argued about Kim.

Rose said, "June doesn't like Zack anymore. So she doesn't care where he is. And she doesn't care who he talks to."

But June did care. She still liked Zack. And she wished she didn't.

Marge said, "It seems as if you still care about Zack, June."

"I don't. Rose told you that," June said.

Marge didn't believe June.

Rose said, "It is almost time for class. We will see you later, Marge."

June and Rose went in the school. But June wasn't in a hurry to get to class.

June had English first. Rose had math.

June hoped Zack wouldn't be in any of her classes this year. But he was in her English class. And so was Kim. Kim was in her history class too.

June asked, "Why does Kim have to be in two of my classes? I have to see her every day in my classes. And I see her every day at practice."

Kim was on the volleyball team too.

"You still don't like Kim, do you?" Rose asked.

"No. I don't like her. And I don't trust her either," June said.

"But it was your fault Zack broke up with you. It wasn't Kim's fault," Rose said.

"I know that," June said.

Kim had eaten lunch with Zack last

year. June found out. She yelled at Kim. She said Kim was trying to take Zack away from her.

But Zack said Kim was only helping him study. And he said June always got mad about nothing. Zack told June to find a new boyfriend.

The girls got to June's class.

Rose said, "I will see you at lunch, June."

"OK," June said.

June went in her class and sat down.

Kim came in and sat down.

Then Zack came in. He sat down next to Kim. They started to talk. And they smiled at each other.

Why did Zack and Kim have to be in her first class? That always got June's day off to a bad start.

Chapter 2

The end of class bell rang. June was glad the class was over. She hurried out of the room. Then she went to her math class. June walked in and sat down.

Marge came in next. She was almost late. She sat down next to June.

Marge said, "I am glad you don't like Zack anymore. I think he and Kim have started dating. What do you think?"

"I don't know who Zack dates. And I don't care," June said.

But June did care.

June had been sure Zack would date Kim last year. But he never did. He had dated other girls. But no one for very long.

But maybe this year Zack and Kim would start to date.

June was glad the bell rang. Then Marge couldn't talk to her.

The class was OK. But June was glad when it was over. She hurried out to her next class. But Kim was in it.

June was glad when it was time for lunch. She was in a hurry to see Rose. Zack had lunch at the same time. But June hoped she wouldn't see him.

June hurried to the lunchroom. Rose waited inside the door. The girls got their trays. Then they went to a table and sat down.

"How was your morning?" Rose asked.

"Not so good," June said.

Rose asked, "Why?"

June said, "Zack and Kim talked to and smiled at each other a lot. Marge thinks they might be dating. Do you think Marge is right?"

Rose said, "Don't listen to Marge. I haven't heard that they are dating. So I don't think they are. But I don't know for sure."

June hoped Rose was right.

The girls ate for a few minutes. And they didn't talk.

But then Rose said, "Zack is looking at you."

That surprised June.

"Maybe he still likes you," Rose said.

"How can you think that? He never talks to me," June said.

Rose said, "I know. But he could still like you."

Zack didn't like her. June was sure about that. It was too late for them.

Rose said, "It has been a long time.

Maybe Zack is sorry about what happened."

"I am sure he is. But that is because of Kim, not me," June said.

"You aren't the same person, June. Maybe Zack will forgive you. He might give you one more chance," Rose said.

"I know Zack. He won't do that," June said.

Rose said, "But maybe he will. You don't lose your temper like you did before."

June had worked hard to control her temper. She had gone to some classes last year. They taught her how to keep control of her temper. June didn't want to go. And she didn't think they would help her. But she knew she needed help. So she went to the classes. The classes helped her a lot. But it hadn't been easy.

Rose said, "I am glad you went to

those classes last year. They helped you a lot. And Zack must know that."

"Do we have to talk about Zack? Can't we talk about something else?" June asked.

"Sure," Rose said.

Rose talked about the Hillman High game. They didn't talk about Zack anymore.

Chapter 3

The rest of the day was OK for June. But she was glad when school was over. June was ready to start the match with Hillman High.

She met Rose at their lockers. Then they hurried to the gym.

The girls quickly got ready to play.

June and Rose were both on the starting team. Their friend Eve was on the starting team too. Kim was on the back-up team.

Carter High had a good starting team. And they had a chance to be number one.

June said, "I am glad Kim isn't on the starting team."

"I know you are, June. You have told me that before," Rose said.

"But Kim doesn't play well. You know that," June said.

Rose said, "Kim can't help how well she plays. And she does play better than she used to."

"Maybe," June said.

But she didn't think Kim played any better. And she didn't think Rose thought so either.

Coach Dale called to June.

She said, "Come over here, June. I need to talk to you."

June walked over to Coach Dale.

Coach Dale said, "The other games were easy wins for us. But Hillman High has a good team. And we might not win this game."

"I know," June said.

Coach Dale said, "I believe you have changed, June. Or you wouldn't be on the team. But I still think I should tell you this again."

June knew what Coach Dale was going to say. But the coach didn't need to tell her again.

"You have only one chance, June. If you lose your temper like you did last year, you are off the team," Coach Dale said.

"I will be OK, Coach Dale. I won't lose my temper," June said.

June had lost her temper in two games last year. She yelled at Kim. But Coach Dale had given her one more chance.

Then June yelled at a referee. Coach Dale took her off the team.

Coach Dale said, "It is time for the game to start. Play your best, June. And don't forget what I said."

"I won't, Coach Dale. You can count on that," June said.

The game started.

Hillman High served first. Hillman High scored three points. But then the Hillman High girl hit her serve out of bounds.

It was Carter High's turn to serve. Rose served first. Rose was the best server on the Carter High team. She had been the best server last year too.

"Put us ahead, Rose. You can do it," June said.

Rose did a good job. And so did the team. Carter High moved ahead 4–3.

Rose served again. Hillman High hit the ball back. But Eve hit the ball out of bounds.

Both teams played well. But Carter High won the first game.

Coach Dale said, "Good game, girls.

Now we need to win the second game."

The second game started.

Eve jumped up to hit a ball. She came down hard on her left foot.

The referee blew his whistle.

June and Rose helped Eve off the court.

Coach Dale asked, "Are you OK,

Eve? Can you play?"

"I don't think so. My foot hurts a lot," Eve said.

Coach Dale said, "Kim, go in and sub for Eve."

Kim went in to play. But she didn't play well.

Carter High lost the second and third game. Hillman High won the match.

June and Rose walked off the court.

June said, "I hope Eve is OK now. She has to play in the Glen High game."

Coach Dale called the team over to her.

She said, "Eve can't play any more this season. So Kim will be on the starting team now."

June couldn't believe it. Why did Eve have to hurt her foot?

June and Rose got ready to go home. Then they walked out of the gym.

June said, "It isn't fair. Why does Kim have to be on the starting team?"

Rose said, "You know why, June. Eve can't play. And Kim is the best player on the back-up team."

June said, "Kim had better learn to play better. Or we will never win again. And we won't have a chance to be number one this year."

June wanted to tell Kim that too.

Rose said, "I wish Coach Dale had more time to help Kim. But she has to help all of the team. Maybe one of us can give Kim some help."

June knew Rose was talking about herself, and not June. There was no way June wanted to help Kim.

She would try not to lose her temper. But she didn't have to help Kim.

Chapter 4

June and Rose were at lunch. It was the day before the Glen High match.

June said, "I have to eat fast."

"Why?" Rose asked.

"I have to go to the media center. I need to find some videos for Mrs. Wayne. I won't have time to go after school," June said.

Mrs. Wayne was her history teacher.

June ate quickly. The girls didn't talk any more. June put her tray up. Then she went to the media center.

Kim was there. But June didn't speak to her.

June looked around. But she

couldn't find what she needed. She walked over to Mrs. Lin. Mrs. Lin was the media center teacher.

June said, "I need some help."

"How can I help you?" Mrs. Lin asked.

June told Mrs. Lin about the videos she needed. Mrs. Lin showed her where they were. Then June went to class.

June didn't see Rose again until after school. They were at volleyball practice.

Rose asked, "Did you find what you needed at the media center?"

"Yes. But Mrs. Lin had to help me find them," June said.

June went for the ball.

Kim came over to them. June just looked at Kim. And June didn't speak to her first.

They weren't friends. So what could Kim want?

Kim said, "I am sorry to bother you, June. But I need your help."

"What for?" June asked.

"I tried to find the videos Mrs. Wayne told us to get. But I couldn't find them. I saw you in the media center. I thought you might have found them. Did you?" Kim asked.

"No," June said.

But that was a lie.

June had to be nice to Kim. And she had to work well with her at practice and at the games. But she didn't have to work with Kim on schoolwork.

Coach Dale called to Kim. Kim hurried over to Coach Dale.

Rose said, "You found what you needed at the media center. So why didn't you tell Kim that?"

"Why should I have?" June asked.

Rose said, "Kim needed some help. And you could have helped her."

"Why should I help her? We aren't friends," June said.

Rose said, "You are better about controlling your temper, June. But you need to learn how to work better with people."

"Thanks, Rose," June said.

But she didn't say it in a nice way.

June said, "I have a problem with my temper. And I need to learn how to work well with people. So what else is wrong with me?"

And June didn't say that in a nice way either.

June was mad. But she couldn't lose her temper.

Coach Dale blew her whistle.

She said, "Time to start."

June was glad it was time to start the practice game. She didn't want to talk to Rose anymore.

Chapter 5

It was the day after the Glen High match. Carter High had lost. And it was because Kim didn't play well.

June was on her way to volleyball practice. Rose was with her.

June said, "We might as well give up now. We shouldn't play any more games."

"Why?" Rose asked.

"We will never win again. Not as long as Kim is on the starting team," June said.

"You don't know that," Rose said.

"Yes, I do," June said.

Rose said, "I will help Kim today. I

think she just needs some extra help. And Coach Dale doesn't have time to give her any extra help."

The girls got to the gym. They quickly got ready to practice. They ran in place for a few minutes. Then they did some stretching exercises.

Coach Dale blew her whistle.

Then she said, "Work on your own for a while. Then we will play some games."

Rose said, "I am going to talk to Kim. I will help her."

But then a girl on the back-up team came over to Rose.

The girl said, "I need some help, Rose. Can you help me for a few minutes?"

"Sure," Rose said.

But now Rose couldn't help Kim.

And Coach Dale was helping someone else.

June looked over at Kim. Kim was working on her serve. But she wasn't doing a good job of it.

Kim needed help. And there was no one else to help her.

June didn't want to help Kim.

But June wanted to win the rest of their matches.

June looked at Kim for a few more minutes. Then she walked over to Kim.

"Need any help?" she asked.

Kim seemed very surprised.

She said, "Sure. I need all the help I can get."

"I will show you how I serve," June said.

June showed Kim how she served.

Then she worked with Kim. And Kim started to serve a little better.

Coach Dale blew her whistle.

She said, "Time to play. Starting team on one side. Back-up team on the other."

Kim said, "Thanks, June. It was very nice of you to help me."

"I will work with you at our next practice too," June said.

But June didn't say that because she was nice.

June still didn't want to help Kim. But she wanted to win. And Kim had to play better, or the team wouldn't win.

Chapter 6

It was the next week. June was in her history class.

Kim came in. She smiled at June. Kim put her books on her desk. Then she walked over to June.

"Thank you for all the help, June," Kim said.

June had helped Kim for three days of practice.

"You don't have to thank me," June said.

"But I do. You didn't have to help me," Kim said.

"I know," June said.

The bell rang. Kim hurried to her desk and sat down.

The students went over their homework.

Then Mrs. Wayne said, "I want you to do a project. You can work on your own. Or you can work with a friend. But no more than two students can work together."

Mrs. Wayne told them more about the project. Then she gave them a list of topics they could choose from.

Then the end of class bell rang.

Kim got up from her desk. She hurried over to June.

She said, "Maybe we could work together on a project."

"Maybe," June said.

June didn't really want to work with Kim. But they could share the work. June wouldn't have to work as hard if she worked with Kim.

Kim said, "We don't have practice

today. So we could meet in the media center after school today. Do you want to do that?"

"OK," June said.

"Great," Kim said.

But June didn't think it was so great. She didn't want to spend more time with Kim. She just wanted less work to do.

The girls quickly picked out a project.

Then Kim said, "See you after school."

"OK," June said.

June was glad it was time for lunch. She went to the lunchroom. She didn't see Rose. She got her tray. Then she went to a table and sat down.

A few minutes later Rose came in. June waved at her.

Rose got her tray. Then she hurried over to the table and sat down.

Rose said, "I saw Kim in the hall. She said she is going to work with you after school. Is that right?"

"Yes," June said.

But June didn't sound like she wanted to do it.

Rose asked, "Aren't you glad to have the help? The work won't take as long."

June said, "I guess. But I still don't trust Kim. And I wonder why she wants to work with me."

"She wants the help. And the work won't take her as long either," Rose said.

June hoped that was why Kim chose to work with her. But she wasn't so sure.

The afternoon went by quickly for June.

The end of school bell rang. June hurried to the media center. She wanted

to get started. Then she could get the work done, and she wouldn't have to work with Kim for very long.

June went in the media center. She looked for Kim. But June didn't see her. Maybe Kim wasn't going to come.

Mrs. Lin walked over to June.

She asked, "Can I help you find something?"

"I am looking for someone," June said.

Then June saw Kim.

June had thought Kim would be sitting by herself. But Kim wasn't by herself.

Kim was sitting with Zack.

Chapter 7

Now June knew why Kim wanted June to meet her. Kim wanted June to see her with Zack. And she wanted June to lose her temper. Then Zack would see that June couldn't control her temper.

Kim saw June. She waved at June. But June didn't go over to the table.

Kim got up from the table. She walked over to June.

It would be hard. But June wouldn't lose her temper.

Kim asked, "What is wrong, June? You seem upset."

"I am upset. But I am not going to

lose my temper. So your plan didn't work," June said.

Kim seemed very surprised.

She asked, "What are you talking about?"

"You know, Kim. And don't act like you don't. I know better," June said.

"I don't know what you are talking about," Kim said.

And Kim didn't seem to know. But June was sure she did.

"You didn't ask me to meet you here to work. You just wanted me to see you with Zack. Then Zack would see me lose my temper. But I told you. I am not going to lose my temper. So your plan didn't work," June said.

"You are wrong, June," Kim said.

"I know better, Kim," June said.

June looked over at Zack. He looked over at them.

June said, "I fell for your act. But now I know what you really want. You just want Zack to see me lose my temper."

But June wouldn't lose her temper.

June went to the door. Then she walked out of the media center.

Kim went after her.

"Wait, June. You have it all wrong," Kim said.

June didn't stop.

"Please wait, June," Kim said.

What was Kim trying to do? Keep after June until she lost her temper?

Other students were looking at them. So June stopped walking. And she waited for Kim.

Kim walked up to her.

She said, "You are wrong, June. I asked Zack to the media center to help you."

Did Kim really think June would believe that? Why would Kim want to help her?

"And just how was that going to help me? Zack isn't in our class," June said.

"But he has some work to do for his class. And I got him to be here now. I was trying to get the two of you back together," Kim said.

That surprised June very much. But she didn't believe Kim.

June said, "I don't believe you. Why would you want to help us get back together?"

"I feel bad about what happened last year," Kim said.

That surprised June very much too.

"Why would you feel bad about it?" June asked.

"You and Zack broke up because of

me. I know it was because I ate lunch with Zack," Kim said.

"But you were helping him with his science," June said.

That was what Zack had told June last year.

Kim said, "But you didn't know that. And that is why you yelled at me. You have helped me a lot this year. And my serves are better now."

June didn't help Kim because she was trying to be nice. She did it to help the team, not Kim.

But she didn't tell Kim that.

"And there is one more reason," Kim said.

"What?" June asked.

Kim said, "I liked a boy last year. And he asked me for a date. But my best friend Fran liked him too. So I didn't date him. Now Fran has moved.

And I would like one more chance with him. But I might not get it. I know how you must feel. I think you should have one more chance with Zack."

June was too surprised to say anything.

Kim said, "Come back in the media center. Study with Zack and me. And maybe Zack will ask you for a date."

June said, "OK. I need to do the work. So I will go back in there."

And maybe it would work out with her and Zack.

But June didn't really think it would.

Chapter 8

June and Kim started to walk back to the media center. June saw Zack. He stood outside the media center door. He looked over at them.

"Hi, Zack," June made herself say.

And she made herself smile at Zack.

"Hi," Zack said.

But he didn't smile at her.

Kim said, "June came to work with me. She thought I was working with you. And I wouldn't have time to work with her. So she left."

Zack didn't say anything. But he seemed surprised.

Kim and June went in the media center. Zack went in behind them.

They walked over to a table. Some books were on the table.

Kim picked up one of the books.

Kim said, "I was reading this book. And I was taking some notes on it. We can share the notes later."

Kim gave a second book to June.

She said, "You can read this book. Or maybe get one from the shelf."

"This one is OK," June said.

They all sat down at the table.

June didn't care what book she read. She cared about only one thing: she was sitting with Zack.

They read for about twenty minutes. And they made some notes.

Then Kim looked at her watch.

She said, "I have to go. I am sorry that I can't stay longer, June. We still have a lot to do. So maybe the two of you could stay and work."

June knew what Kim was trying to do. She wanted June and Zack to be at the same table. With no one else there, maybe Zack would talk to June. And maybe he would ask June for a date.

But Zack might go too.

Kim looked at both of them.

June waited for Zack to say something. But he didn't.

So June said, "I can stay."

But would Zack stay with her?

At first Zack didn't say anything. But then he said, "I have a lot more to do. So I guess I can stay for a while."

"Great," Kim said.

She had a big smile on her face.

Kim quickly got up from the table. She picked up her books.

"See you in class tomorrow," Kim said.

Then Kim hurried out of the media center.

June acted as if she was reading her book. But she wasn't at all.

Zack acted as if he was reading his book. But June wasn't sure that he was.

They sat there for about ten minutes.

Zack and June didn't talk. Kim's plan wasn't working.

But this might be June's only chance to talk to Zack. They would have to leave the media center soon. So June knew she had to say something.

"It was nice of Kim to ask me to study with her," June said.

Zack seemed surprised.

He said, "Yeah. It was nice of her. But she is a nice person."

"I know," June said.

They sat for a few more minutes. And they didn't talk.

Then June said, "I am glad you could stay."

Zack didn't say anything.

Mrs. Lin said, "The media center will close in ten minutes. So you must be ready to go."

Most of the students quickly left.

June said, "Maybe the three of us could study English together some time."

"Maybe," Zack said.

"Or maybe just the two of us could," June said.

Zack seemed very surprised.

He said, "I don't know about that."

Was Zack dating someone? Or didn't he want to study with her? June had to know. And there was only one way to find out. She had to ask Zack. So she made herself ask him.

She asked, "Are you dating someone now?"

At first Zack didn't answer.

But then he said, "No."

June made herself say more.

"Will you give me one more chance?" June asked.

"I gave you a lot of chances last year," Zack said.

June said, "I know. But I am not like I was last year. I don't lose my temper like I did then."

Zack didn't say anything.

Mrs. Lin said, "The media center will close in five minutes."

June knew it was too late for her and Zack. So she got up to go.

Then Zack said, "Kim said you have been very nice to her this year. She said you helped her at practice. So OK."

"OK what?" June asked.

"I will give you one more chance, June. But only one more. Lose your temper one time like you did last year, and we are over for good," Zack said.

June couldn't believe it. Zack would give her one more chance. And it was because she had been nice to Kim.

June would show Zack that she was not the same girl. She wouldn't lose her temper. And this time, she wouldn't lose Zack.